I am Flippish!

Written by Leslie V. Ryan
Illustrated by Adolph Soliz

D1534418

Text Copyright © 2008 Leslie V. Ryan
Illustrations Copyright © 2011 by Leslie Ryan
All rights reserved.

First edition 2011

Library of Congress Cataloging – in – Publication Data
Leslie V. Ryan

TXu 1-660-852

ISBN: 1460930320
ISBN 13: 9781460930328

This book would not have been made without the amazing support of my family and friends.

Thank you!

WITHDRAWN

Sean was a happy 7 year old boy who loved school. Every Tuesday Mom helped out in his classroom. Sean loved Tuesdays with his mom. One day, Mom came down with a cold and had to send Dad to help out instead.

4

Sean was so proud and excited to have Dad help out in his classroom for the first time. When Sean introduced his dad to his classmates, one boy James exclaimed, "You can't be Sean's dad, you have white skin – Sean has brown skin. You have yellow hair, and Sean has black hair!" Then the other kids started to ask questions.

"How come Sean doesn't look like you?" said Samantha.

"He looks like his Mom," said Nicole.

"Is Sean adopted? I'm adopted," said Mark.

Sean started to feel very sad. This was his dad! Why were they saying he did not look like Dad? Mom said he had Dad's smile and eyebrows and her dimples and tanned skin. He got a little bit of everything from Mom and Dad. *"Maybe having Dad help in class was not a great idea after all,"* he thought.

Mr. Hartman clapped his hands and announced, "Alright class, for your homework tonight, I want you to ask your parents what country your ancestors came from. An ancestor is a family member such as your grandmother, grandfather, and their parents and so on and so forth. You will be surprised with what you find out."

That night during dinner of rice, chicken adobo (a Filipino stew), peas, and toffee pudding, Sean asked Mom and Dad about why he didn't look like Dad.

Mom said, "Sean, you are half Filipino and half Irish! You are Flippish, which is short for Filipino Irish."

Dad added, "Sean, you got the best of our features. That is why you look like you do."

Sean's 3 year old sister Linley, chimed in, "I look like Mommy! I am Mommy's mini-me!"

"And you, Linley, got Mom's face, and my blue eyes!" said Dad.

14

"We are Flippish!" yelled Sean and Linley.

After dinner Dad showed Sean a map of the world. He pointed to Ireland and said, "Sean, my Dad -- your grandpa -- sailed to America from Ireland to find his fortune just like millions of people who came from around the world to America. Your Nana's Mom came from Ireland too! However, Nana was born in San Francisco where I was born."

Sean's Mom said, "My parents, your Nanay and Papa, came from the Philippines which is located on the other side of the world in a place called Asia. But I met your Dad here in America, got married and had you and your sister."

"So that's why I'm Flippish," Sean said with a smile.

"Let's play a game. Your Uncle Pedro is from Argentina and your Auntie Noreen is Irish which makes your cousins Joe and Brendan..." Mom asked.

"Argentish?" said Sean.

"Yes!" exclaimed Mom.

"Let's try another one! Our neighbor Mr. Gonzalez is Mexican and Mrs. Gonzalez is Japanese, so Haley is…"

"Japsican…?" asked Sean, after taking a few minutes to think about it.

"Very good Sean!" said Mom.

21

Sean went to bed happy, whispering to himself, "I am Flippish, I am Flippish…"

The next day, Mr. Hartman asked the class where their ancestors came from. He asked Sean first.

"My Dad is Irish and my Mom is Filipino, so I am Flippish!" he said with a smile.

Grant raised his hand and said, "My Mom is Scottish and my Dad is also Filipino, so what does that make me?"

Sean thought about it and said, "You are Flottish!"

Everybody laughed.

James shouted out, "But you have yellow hair and white skin, you cannot be like Sean who has black hair and brown skin."

Sean said, "My Mom and Dad said that I was made from their best parts! Grant, you got your Mom and Dad's best parts!"

"My neighbor's Mom and Dad are Japanese and Mexican, so my friend Haley is Japsican!" declared Sean.

28

Soon, everybody stood up and told the class where their parents came from and worked together to come up with names.

William was Vietalian for Vietnamese Italian,

Nicole was Permenian for Persian Armenian,

Paolo was Candranian for Canadian Ukranian,

Tanner was Jamerindian for Japanese American-Indian,

James was Swenglish for Swedish English,

Ava was Maltralian for Maltese Australian,

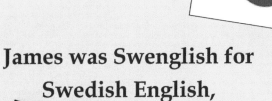

29

Samantha was Sofringlish for
South African English,

Holden was Norwexican for
Norwegian Mexican,

Sebastian was
Frindonesian for
French Indonesian,

Rahul was Srilandian for
Sri Lankan Indian,

Hailey was Guarman for
Guatemalan German,

Colin was Japenglish for
Japanese English,

Eva was Kortalian for
Korean Italian,

Adolph was Indixican for
American Indian Mexican,
And finally,

Mr. Hartman was Italman for
Italian German.

Everybody had a fun time helping each other come up with names. Sean was very pleased.

"Our 44th President's father was from Kenya and his mother was from Kansas whose ancestors were English, what does that make President Obama?" asked Mr. Hartman.

"Kenglish?" answered Holden.

"How about Kenican for Kenyan and American?" asked Rahul.

Mr. Hartman said, "You are both right. See, class, we are a mix of different people and cultures. They make us who we are. Just because you don't look like your Mom or Dad does not make it wrong. We are all made up of the best parts of our parents."

With that, there were no more questions on why somebody looks different from their parents, except for Mark who is adopted and that is another story.

Sean found out he was Flippish, what are you?

33

My Ancestors came from:

_____

_____

_____

_____

_____

Therefore I am:

_____

_____

_____

_____

_____

About the Author

Leslie V. Ryan graduated from University of California, at Berkeley with a bachelor's degree in Legal Studies and Japanese Language. Her love for books began when she started reading at a young age of four and that love still continues today. Recently, the passion for reading books turned into a newfound love of writing them. She lives with her husband, and "Flippish" son and daughter in Southern California.

About the Illustrator

A graduate from The Laguna College of Art and Design with a BFA in animation, Adolph Soliz who is "Indixican", brings charming and endearing characters to life in all media. Which means you'll never find him without his sketchbook, observing the world and people around him. Over the years he has done work for Disney and other companies. Along with illustrating children's books he also teaches art to young aspiring artists.

3 1901 05767 5615

Made in the USA
Charleston, SC
07 June 2016

57191015R10023